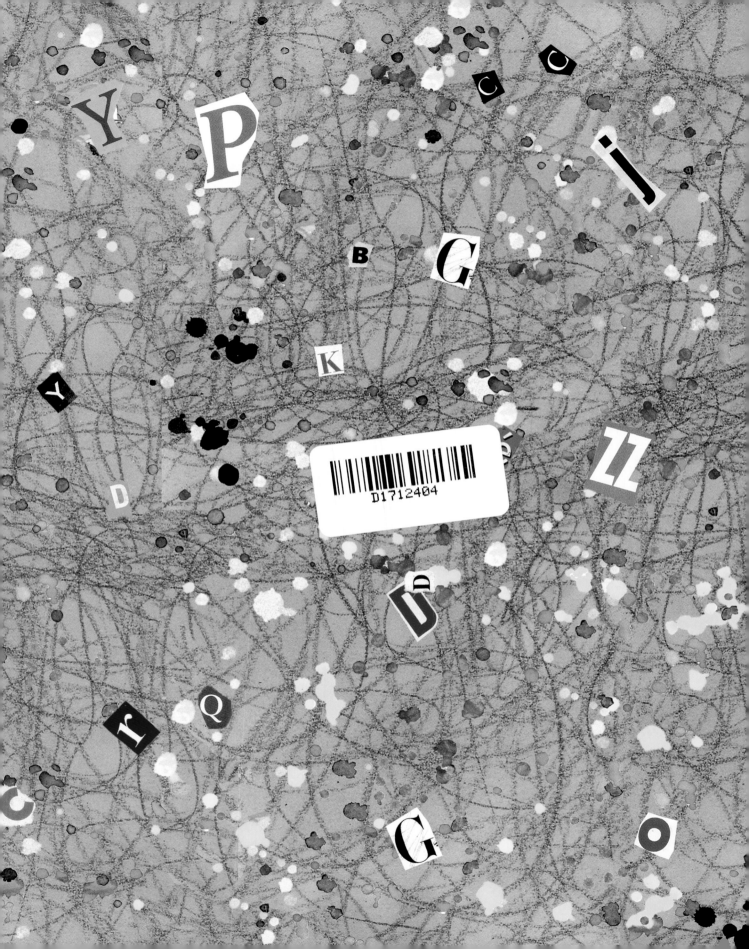

Paule Brière

The Undesirables

Illustrations by Philippe Béha

SIMPLY READ BOOKS

Published in 2008 by Simply Read Books
www.simplyreadbooks.com
First published by Les 400 Coups
Text © 2006 Paule Brière
Illustrations © 2006 Philippe Béha

LIBRARY AND ARCHIVES CANADA CATALOGUING IN PUBLICATION
Brière, Paule
[Indésirables. English]
   The undesirables / Paule Brière ; illustrations, Philippe Béha.

Translation of: Les indésirables.
ISBN 978-1-894965-88-0

   I. Béha, Philippe II. Title.

PS8553.R453515313 2008   jC843'.54   C2008-901247-X

We gratefully acknowledge for their financial support of our publishing
program the Canada Council for the Arts, the BC Arts Council, and
the Government of Canada through the Book Publishing Industry
Development Program (BPIDP).

Book design by Elisa Gutiérrez

10 9 8 7 6 5 4 3 2 1

Printed in Singapore

For Custer, Hitler, Pol Pot, Khomeini and Milosevic, and for the true undesirables of today in the hope that someday they may understand.

And for Marc, who told me this story.

Paule

ONCe upon a time

there lived a queen and
a king. In their kingdom
lived all sorts of subjects.
Some were agreeable
and others were not so
agreeable.

The queen and the king were not satisfied with the quality of their subjects. They dreamed of a perfect kingdom. They called for their Granvilan.

"Lock up all the undesirables!" they ordered.

The Granvilan was a little troubled. "The undesirables?" he said. "Uh . . . of course, your Majesties. But . . . which ones?"

Lock up all the undesirables!

The king and queen shouted,

everything in this kingdom!

And so they made a list of all those they wanted imprisoned.

First, they identified the

Archprickilys

and the **Babbilylips**.

These subjects were unquestionably
undesirables!

They continued with the **Crumpitycrocs,** the **Dododungs** and the **Eggilydice.**

Certainly these subjects, too, were unacceptable!

When night fell, they listed the Idiototos, the Jitterjabs.

and the Kaptables.

During the night they added the

Malameeps,
the Naselnarks,
the Oogleoafs
and the
Quaquapouettes.

Before dawn their list included the

Richyfries,

the Stinklestars,

the Tappitytwits

and the Uglepuffs.

The longer the list grew, the more the Granvilan wondered,

Where are we going to put all these undesirables? The dungeon is not big enough.

Finally the king and the queen concluded
with the

Wallopwailers,

the Xenoblinks,

the Yukayokes

and the

Zoozles.

The list of the kingdom's undesirables was finished. Not a single subject was spared, not even the Granvilan!

When he read his name between the Fimbleforks and the Higglidyspoons, the Granvilan made a grave decision.

He wasn't going to make the dungeon bigger or construct a new one.
He had a better solution.

He called together the

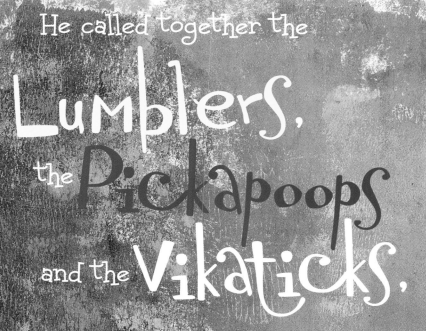

Lumblers,
the Pickapoops
and the Vikaticks,

who were not the most pleasant
subjects but always willing to do a
favor for the Granvilan.

While the queen and the king were sleeping the Granvilan and his accomplices dug deep moats around the castle—moats impossible to cross, moats without drawbridges to cross them.

When the king and the queen
woke up, their kingdom was
as perfect as the desert.

Finally the true undesirables
were locked away.

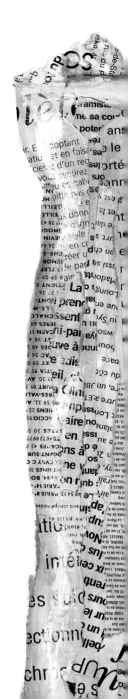

That taught them to be intolerant,

those intolera

bleʃ!

The End

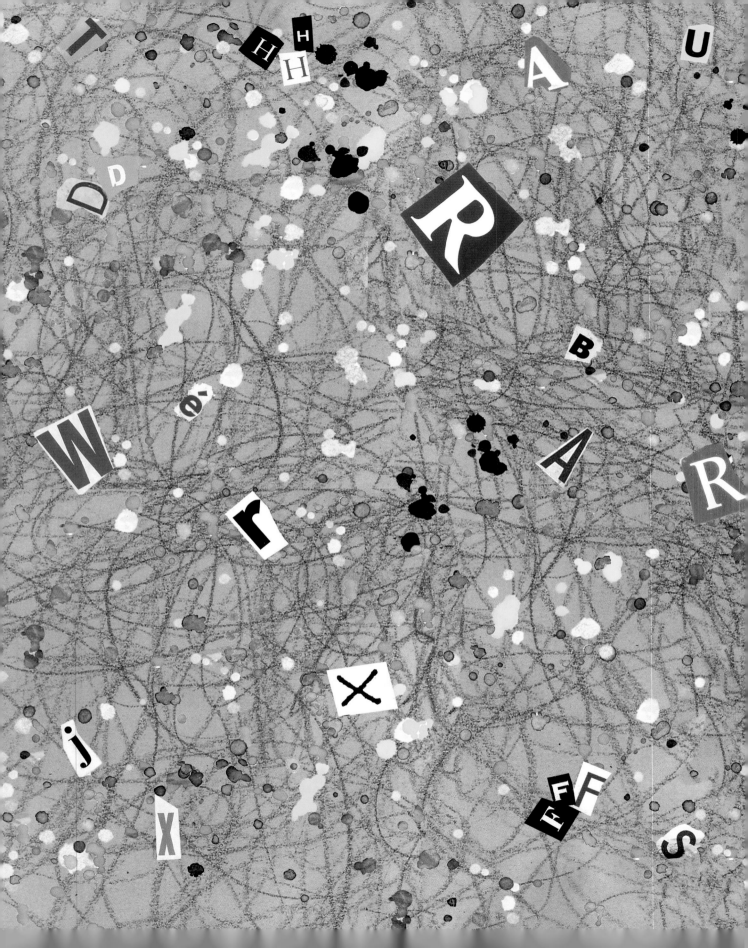